for my Grandmother
Edna Williams,
my daughter Akasa,
my sons Sierra and Nkoya,
and my granddaughter
Isabella

First Edition August 2014

EXPRESSIVE ARTS PRODUCTIONS

Edited by Carol A.Pitt

ISBN: 978-150-0492-42-7   (paperback)

This Too Will Pass

Sonia S. Williams

To Carol.

Ubuntu I am because you are
you are because I am

Enjoy Reading

JH April. 2015

With thanks to all those who helped me grow and supported my artistic development, Birchmore Griffith, Walter and Cynthia Bailey, Margaret Headley, Walter Bailey, Carl Taylor, Sierra Williams-Bailey, Audrey Lynch, Gary Cole, Ryan Headley, Stafford Ashani, Carol A. Pitt, Rawle Gibbons, Kamau Brathwaite, Erna Brodber, Icil Phillips, the creator, the celestial energies and all the ancestors.

1

The year was long before you were born. My grandmother Dolly, who was your great-great-grandmother, was a young girl at the time. Something in the water was killing the people. Mothers use to go to work and come back and find their children dead dead dead, but every one of Dolly's mother Vee ten children live through the ordeal. Vee had the secret, she use to extract water from the ground provisions."

"But how she do that Gran?" Amanda asked.

"Don't ask me how. That is when the rumor spread that Vee use to dabble, but Dolly knew she mother was a God-fearing woman. Your great-great-great-grandmother Vee knew things other people didn't know, that is all."

Gran eased all the way back against the strips of the blue and white vinyl beach chair and shifted her feet in the warm water.

"What things Gran?" Amanda asked.

Gran looked out at the sky, burnt orange with the evening sun. Her face opened up and she smiled.

"At that time there was a man named Strappings. Think of a bulldozer pushing down a tree, well that was Strappings as a young boy. The man could cut more canes in one day than the fancy machines they got 'bout here now, and you use to get a better quality harvest. Strappings was shiny black until he was blue, and tall like a bamboo tree. You hardly see people sweet black so in these parts these days. When he smile, his eyes use to shine and light up his whole face like the full moon at night. Everybody liked Strappings, but it was Bernita's daughter Violet that win his heart."

Gran took a deep breath and looked off

into the distance. Amanda watched Gran's forehead wrinkle, the bulges of brown skin like the ridges of an ant's nest. She sighed.

"The sad thing is she couldn't have children. Violet was barren."

Gran's silence grew heavy. A fly made a circle in front of her face.

"Gran, what happen?" Amanda asked.

"Damn fly, the rains soon come. Go inside and bring the fly swatter let me kill he."

"But Gran…" Amanda groaned.

"Go and bring the thing girl. These two old feet tired, my time soon come."

"Stop saying so Gran."

"When it is my time it is my time." Gran answered.

Amanda opened the door. The presence of the spirit of the night had already entered the room, her shadows making the dust of the day shine like glitter over the deep browns of the mahogany chairs, with their rich burgundy and deep green flowered cushions. She stood in awe of the night's presence, forgetting why she had entered the room in the first place.

"What you frighten for?" Gran asked.

"I not frightened!" Amanda shouted as she dashed through the front house, past the mahogany dining table and into the kitchen.

"Look on the kitchen counter Mandy!" Gran shouted.

"I know Gran!" Amanda shouted back.

Amanda made the decision that the spirit of the night could not turn her to glitter, picked up her two feet, and ran as fast as she could to the gallery. The fly made circles of sound in front of Gran's face, making a final landing on the yellow railing of the gallery. Gran smashed it with the fly swatter and pushed its black carcass over the edge.

Amanda extended her spine, her upper torso hanging over the railing, watching the falling fly's last glow disappearing in the creeping presence of the night. *The spirit of the night got that one*, she thought.

"Finish the story Gran," Amanda pleaded. "Finish the story."

Amanda sat crossed-legged at Gran's feet

looking up at her face. Gran's lips quivered.

"Well, one Friday afternoon the church bell start to ring like mad. Everybody stop work and run up the side of the hill. Strappings drop down dead in the middle of the field. The men shake Strappings from side to side. They throw water in his face, put smelling salts under his nose, but Strappings would not move. Everybody start to panic causing nobody can hear his heartbeat. They send for Doctor Yearwood. He come and declare Strappings legally dead. Some people say it was sunstroke, other people say it must be the water, causing everybody know work never kill nobody yet.

"Back then there was no deep freeze to keep the body, so burials use to happen by the next day. Dorphus, Strappings' uncle on his father side, put the body on the donkey cart and carry Strappings home. Mrs. Sobers give him a bath with mulberry and balsam and laid him in the inner room with all the curtains drawn. The only mirror in the house and the drum was covered by black cloth. Tin Tin build a deal wood coffin for Strappings and Violet prepare he only suit for the burial. Violet just couldn't believe it… after all Strappings eat he breakfast and left home good good the morning, no complaints, no pain nowhere, now he… she couldn't say the word. Violet drink a shot of Arthur white rum to calm she nerves."

Gran paused and leaned forward, tapping each side of her right leg, then each side of her left leg, and then holding each leg by the knee, she lifted them one by one out of the water. Amanda rubbed the stone Gran had taken from the sea on the rough edges of Gran's feet which had gone soft and white from the long soak. Layers of dead skin flaked, fell and dissolved in the Epsom salts water.

Amanda dried Gran's ankles as well as between and underneath the creases of her toes with a big blue towel, and oiled her feet with glycerin.

"Thank you Lord Jesus!" Gran released the praise on a breathy sigh as she resettled her body in the chair.

"You don't know about those days, Mandy, those were mysterious days. You had to be patient in those days. Those were the days of horse and buggy, chile. You don't know 'bout those days. Everybody in white for funerals, not black, and if a child pass way the buggy in white too. A funeral was pure singing in those days. Friends and relations walking from the night before to get to the house, the body laid out in the front house and everybody singing. No funeral parlor, burial was a personal thing."

Amanda's focus shifted from Gran's feet to her face, radiant in the evening's light. Gran's voice became rich and strong.

"Well, before the sun reach the center of the sky and embrace the earth like young lovers, the procession was ready to leave Rose Hill to go up to All Saints Church. The mourners' singing, heavy and severe, filled the hillside. When the driver guide the horse and buggy round Rose Hill corner to go up Benn Hill road the coffin shift in the back of the cart. The driver stop the buggy. Tallies, Strappings' uncle on his mother side, couldn't find anything wrong with the donkey cart or the coffin. Tallies and the driver shift the coffin back to the center of the cart and start back on the journey. Your great, great, great grandmother Vee called the song, her voice quivered over the heads of the community of mourners.

Abide with me fast falls the even tide,
The darkness deepens Lord with me abide.

"The community answered, their voices stretching with the pain of Strappings' sudden passing. Violet emptied her belly of the grief. The wail ricocheted off the hot tar road, echoing in the living rooms of the small chattel houses, swinging open back doors, flying over the tops of palings through winding alleys, sending many running to the sidewalk to open the way for Strappings. The singing so sweet, you could feel God right there amongst the people, making villagers who didn't plan to come to the funeral join the procession to the church."

Gran raised her hand just above her head, feeling God's presence, reaching for the unseen. Amanda could hear the song in her head clear, like the procession was happening right in front of the gallery. Gran looked out towards the horizon. The last quarter of the sun had been consumed by the sea. Darkness was spreading her arms across the edge of the world. Amanda pulled her knees into her chest and hugged herself. Gran continued the story, her eyes still focused off in the distance as the sun fell over the edge.

"Halfway up Benn Hill the coffin start rocking and the buggy start shaking. The driver stop the horse and buggy. The singing pause as some of the mourners drift back, afraid. Vee walked right up to the buggy and climbed on top. Tallies and the driver join Vee on top of the buggy to see what was wrong. The coffin continued to rock from side to side. The driver jump off the cart and run, but Vee and Tallies stand their ground.

You know when Tallies manage to open the coffin, Strappings sit right up covering his eyes with his hands. Vee help he to stand, causing he was weak in the knees. Everybody says that your great-great-great grandmother Vee knew no fear. She was a spiritual woman."

"But how do you know it happened Gran, you did not witness it?" Amanda asked, looking directly into Gran's eyes.

"It isn't everything you have to see to believe and what you see sometimes is not what it appears to be," Gran answered. "After all, did the sun just fall into the sea?"

"No Gran," Amanda answered, "it just look so."

Amanda was silent. It was the time of the day she liked the most. She could see change happening before her eyes. Darkness was here now; she wore a long robe that was limitless like the waters of the sea. The fruit trees, dull shadows of their daytime bodies, grew heavy, gathering themselves into bundles with the weight of her garment.

Amanda did not trust the darkness. She was like a trickster undoing all that was done in the day.

In the quiet of the night she thought of the old chattel house taken apart at the crack of dawn at Pleasant Hall where they used to live, and put back together by sunset in Mile and a Quarter, where they lived now. They had moved right after Amanda's birthday. She remembered because Gran said the house was in a state because of packing, so she couldn't have a birthday party. Gran said she would have a party for her next birthday. It felt safe in this new house with its bright light bulbs in the night. She thought of the heavy, dark nights at Pleasant Hall: the chattel house on the bank of stone with its grey shingled windows closed to the world outside, the two limestone steps at the door on which Amanda sat and looked across to the bank on the other side of the road at the fourteen steps of All Saints Boy's school, grey with age, the big mahogany tree with roots like the veins of a working man's hand, the church, the graveyard, and the spirits. Oh there were spirits! Amanda used to feel their presence and hear them.

Amanda moved closer to Gran and laid the side of her head on Gran's lap. Amanda had never told Gran she heard spirits. She would lie on the patches of grass between the roots of the mahogany tree rising out of the earth for hours, her body pressed against the ground, listening. She could feel their rhythms spiraling through her veins, making her heart race. When she first heard the whispers from the other side her heart dropped into her belly and she was pulled through the hole by the vibrations of the sound.

Amanda thought she had died and was surprised when she woke up to find her body soaking wet, exhausted, and Gran standing over her like the sky. She could not move. At first she never remembered what happened when she came back. She just felt like a space inside her had opened up and could see and feel more.

"Amanda, you sleeping?"

Gran's voice brought her back to the gallery and the night. She felt a breeze brush against the back of her neck and down the back of her arm. She heard the crickets rubbing their legs together.

"No Gran. I studying."

"What you got to study?"

"The mahogany tree."

"By the boys school?"

"Yes Gran, that tree got spirits."

"What you know about spirits?"

"I know the trees down here different."

Gran looked at Amanda's eyes. From the day she was born Gran knew she was an old spirit. It was the presence of light in her eyes, the knowing.

"Let we go inside Gran."

"You frighten for the night?" Gran challenged.

"No! But sometimes at night the clothes hanging in the bedroom does look like duppies. I don't want to go in there by myself."

"The dead can't do you a thing. It is the living you have to watch for."

"Gran, let we go inside nuh?" Amanda pleaded.

"You go child. You go. I going soak in the night." Gran answered, rubbing Amanda gently on the crown of her head. But Amanda would not budge, not without Gran.

I going soak in the night too, Amanda thought to herself. *I going soak in the night.*

2

"Hiddy my diddy my master's gold ring
Come from the back and front again
Who stole my master's gold ring?
Come Jack, come Jack
For your master's gold ring
Shut up your lap tight tight tight tight"

Amanda, Cathy and Michelle sang at the tops of their voices on the plateau of Mount Brevitor Hill in Mile and a Quarter. The pace of their song increased as their hands, balled into fists, moved from lap to lap. Sophia was hiding behind the big rock they called the rock of Gibraltar. They kept their facial expressions neutral, trying not to laugh, yet not to be too serious. No one wanted to be caught with the master's gold ring.

At the end of the song Sophia rushed in from behind the rock of Gibraltar. She would have to choose whose fist was holding the pebble posing as the master's gold ring. Amanda, Cathy and Michelle sat still, their legs squeezed together, their hands balled into fists, their eyes blank, thinking nothing so Sophia would not guess who was hiding the smooth pebble posing as the 'master's gold ring'.

Sophia turned up her face like she smelled sour water from clothes left soaking for days. She shook her index finger in the face of each girl, with a look in her eyes like she already knew who had the master's gold ring.

Cathy, in trying not to laugh, let out a sound like the whizzing of a cat. Sophia shouted "Cathy!" and pointed her fingers at Cathy's lap where her hands laid folded in a ball. Cathy said, "No-oooooooo!" stretching the sound long to increase Sophia's torture.

"Amanda! Amanda!" Gran's voice echoed across the field and up to the top of the hill where the girls sat.

How Gran knows it is me? Amanda thought to herself, squeezing her eyebrows together and saying nothing. Michelle stayed absolutely still, determined to win.

Gran turned off the stove and moved quickly to the back door while wiping her hands on the bottom corner of her apron. She placed her head through the wooden window held up in the corner by a stick and bawled, "Amanda!!! Amanda!!!"

Sophia looked each girl in the eye, her head turning from left to right, then right to left and left to right again. Amanda did not flinch. Even Gran's voice could not make her give a sign that she was the one with the master's gold ring.

Gran pulled up the latch and the big yellow door swung open.

"Where that child gone now nuh?" Gran stepped onto the top steps, hand akimbo, faced the hill, took a deep breath, and like a drum, bellowed: "AMANDA! AMANDA!"

As the sound reached the top of the hill where the girls sat, Sophia shouted, "Amanda!"

"COMING GRAN!" Amanda answered, ignoring Sophia's glare.

"You got it! I know you got it!" Sophia rushed to Amanda and tried to pull Amanda's fist open.

"Not fair! You only know causing Gran call me." Amanda squeezed her fist tighter.

"Not! I win fair and square." Sophia insisted.

"Yes! If Gran didn't call me, you wouldn't have known!" Amanda shouted.

"Not!"

"Yes!"

"Not!"

"Yes!"

"AMANDA! AMANDA!"

"COMING GRAN!"

"AMANDA!"

"COMING!"

"AMANDA!"

"COMING!"

"STOP COMING AND COME!"

The words traveled through a tunnel of time that made Amanda, Sophia, Michelle, Gran, the birds, the trees, all of Mount Brevitor Hill, even the wind, stand still in reverence. Amanda became intensely aware of her body and everything around her being alive and connected …then everybody caught themselves. A flock of birds flew up into the sky, the wind rustled in the trees and Amanda threw the pebble at Sophia's feet.

"I got to go, Gran calling me."

"See!" Sophia shouted as she jumped back and pointed at the pebble lying where her feet stood a moment earlier. "And you almost hit my foot with that rock stone."

But it was too late for a fight. Amanda was already gone, moving like light, riding on a tunnel of sound on a passageway created by feet over time, ducking under overhanging branches extending overhead, turning limestone corners with black sage and grass that jutted out and hid what was on the other side; down the steep slippery path skipping over rock; feet hardly touching the ground; fast, free, fearless. Downhill, passing around the belly of the limestone quarry and past the three big sugar apple trees until her feet touched the flat ground.

Gran, seeing Amanda in the distance, hustled back to the kitchen. Amanda skipped down the pathway between Gran's land and Sophia's grandmother's land, past the family of banana trees to the back gate. Pushing her body against the heavy galvanized door, she eased it forward, placed her tiny finger through the space under the latch and lifted it. The door creaked open.

Gran's voice echoed from inside: "Latch it back," in anticipation of its annoying, slow swing in the wind, the chickens getting out, and the utter confusion that could follow having to catch them one by one.

Gran specialized in seeing things before they happened and making sure they did not happen with the grace of God. Gran could even tell when death was coming. The message came to her in a dream, in a vision, or in how the dogs barked at night.

Her appearance at the back step to check if the gate was locked and the state of Amanda was no surprise. Gran stood like God would on the final day surveying the candidate for judgment.

"You didn't hear me calling you?" Gran demanded.

Amanda bowed her head and looked at her feet, anxiously placing her left big toe on top of her right big toe and rubbing the bottom on the top.

She looked up. "Yes Gran."

"So why you now come?"

Amanda rubbed the other four toes vigorously with the back of her feet.

"I'm sorry Gran."

Amanda shifted her body from the spot and looked down to see where the ants came from. She did not recall seeing an ant's nest in that area of the yard.

"But look how long it took you to come."

Gran tilted her head to the side as her eyes reached across the yard and touched Amanda in her belly.

Yes, she had heard Gran calling and yes, she had taken her time coming. She placed her arms on top of her head, crossing them at the wrist.

"Take your hands off your head, your mother not dead. Wash your feet and come inside and get something to eat before the sun go down."

Gran swung her hips and was gone. Amanda tiptoed around the chickens, over the chicken doo-doo and washed her feet at the yard pipe.

"Macaroni pie an' chicken wing, that is all I want."

She sang the lyrics to a calypso rhythm out loud, letting the sound of the words shape the melody, the pangs of hunger choosing the places of emphasis. *"Macaroni pie an' chicken wing, that is all I want. Macaroni pie an' chicken wing that is all I want."*

The chickens ran around the yard, pecking

at the ground, jerking their heads in time as if dancing to Amanda's melody. The wing of the chicken was the only part of the chicken she would eat since she saw Gran kill one of the chickens.

Gran had filled up the aluminum tub with hot water. She held the chicken body in one hand, the head in the other, and with one twist, chicken head in one direction and chicken body in the other direction, removed the chicken's head. Thin, long streams of blood squirted from the chicken's neck as its body jerked and quivered. Gran soaked it in hot water and plucked its feathers.

Amanda stood on top of the step watching Gran's every move, tears running down her cheekbones. She ate no chicken that Sunday since she saw the blood running from its neck and saw life leaving the flesh, white like hers when she got cut by a knife once. The next chicken she ate came from the deep freeze in the supermarket. It had no head. She ate the wing. That part of the chicken had so little flesh and she could taste the sweetness of Gran's seasoning.

"*Macaroni pie and chicken wing, Gran seasoning in between. Macaroni pie and chicken wing, Gran seasoning in between.*"

Singing louder, knees bent, hands propped on her knees, bottom tilted back, Amanda made full circles with her waist, twisting her head so that she could see her bottom swirl and stick on "*...tween, Macaroni pie and chicken wing, Gran seasoning in between.*"

Amanda walked up the top steps and looked up at Mount Brevitor Hill, its limestone belly carved out. The girls were gone now, but the mile trees were still reaching for the sky, their tips bending in the wind. It looked like a mystical place, the hilltop.

"Amanda! Come before the food get cold." Gran called from inside the yellow house.

"Coming Gran! Coming!"

Amanda loved the yellow house in Mile and a Quarter. It had an indoor toilet and electricity, not like the house at Pleasant Hall.

3

Pleasant Hall was plantation land. *Ebbath*, the plantation house, sat at the highest point on the savannah-like hill surrounded by fields and fields of sugar cane, reaching up and across so much they seemed to reach the end of the earth.

By the time Amanda was born nobody wanted to work in the cane fields. Gran used to work at one plantation or the next from the time she was eight years old. One vacation Gran's mother, Nannie, sent her to work in the Third Gang cutting pond grass, and she never went back to school. Back then Gran used to get eight cents at the end of the week.

When Gran was old enough she worked heading the cane bundles to the truck. Gran did all sorts of work, from digging potatoes at Bissex, St. Andrew, to mixing mortar to build the big house by St. Lucy's Parish Church. That is how she met Vernon and had her first child Gloria. But that didn't work out, because he had already married a woman whom he kept in a house in Belleplaine.

Then Gran met Ebert the tractor driver. Ebert had four children when he met Gran, three boys and one girl, all from one woman. He married Gran and had three girls. One died in the crossing over, and two lived: Thelma and Amanda's mother Ann. Gran raised all six children, three boys and three girls.

Ebert died before Amanda was born when a tractor fell on him and crushed his legs. Amanda never knew what he looked like. They say if he was alive Amanda would never have been born. He was very strict and believed in the power of the rod. Even Gran used to feel his hand sometimes. He died three weeks after the accident.

Gran said that after the doctor cut off the minced flesh that was once his means of support and transport and left him legless, he released his spirit and refused to live. She was sorry he died, but it was his time and she was glad he didn't have to suffer long.

Gran never had another man. She kept the metal plate they put on his coffin in the top drawer of her dresser, where she kept her I.D. card, her box with her beads and brooches, and her Holy Bible—King James version. Some days Amanda would go into her drawer and finger the shiny silver plate, rubbing it with the wrong side of the bottom of her dress, trying to touch him through the letters of his name, rubbing it, looking at her reflection, reading it over and over again:

REST IN PEACE
EBERT DA COSTA WILSON
BORN JULY 6TH 1912-DIED NOVEMBER 14TH 1962
Rest in Peace.

Too many cane fires caused Gran to move from Pleasant Hall. For what seemed like forever Gran and Thelma packed everything into a big trunk, cardboard boxes, big traveling bags, crocus bags, and every kind of container they could find. Early one Saturday morning men came, took the chattel house apart, packed it on the back of a lorry, and Gran moved down the hill to Mile and a Quarter.

Gran's great auntie Catherine had died and left her a plot of land through a gap with a big tamarind tree at the bottom in Mile and a Quarter. The plot started a quarter of the way up the gap behind Auntie Catherine's house, and ended at the bottom of Mount Brevitor Hill right by the mouth of the quarry.

Gran knew it was a gift from God. Gran talked to him every morning about everything on her mind. As soon as she awoke her knees would find the floor. She would lean all her weight into the bed, raise her hands to the sky, and pray. Gran would pray constantly. Bending over the jukking board in the yard washing, her hands hovering just as high as they could reach, God would send shivers through Gran that shocked her system, making her head jerk back and roll to the side. Gran would launch into a prayer:

"Thank you Lord Jesus. Only you know what it is year after year them burning the canes, and you house in the middle of the fields. But you won't send more than I could bear. I put it in your hands sweet Jesus. I laid my burdens at your feet and you answered the call. Thank you Lord Jesus. You are the Great Redeemer. Thank you Lord. Thank you Jesus."

Then God would bend Gran's back over, and her hands would start rubbing the clothes with elbow grease that made the clothes sing. Gran would raise a song of praise until all the clothes were washed and the clothes lines were laden. With the help of God and money sent in from the three boys who went to England and two girls who went to America, the house was expanded from four to eight rooms, a bathroom with a shower and an indoor toilet, a big kitchen and a gallery facing the West Coast, painted a bright and shiny yellow. The yellow house stood in the center of clusters of families of trees: breadfruit, gooseberry, coconut, mango, paw-paw, ackee, and banana trees.

Auntie Thelma planted Joseph's coat, hibiscus, lilies, ferns and poinsettias outside the front gallery. On the edge of the garden was a golden apple tree so close you could climb on the ledge of the gallery and pick ripe, juicy golden apples.

Behind Auntie Catherine's house was a Bajan cherry tree with a huge afro and a clammacherry tree with a bee hive bush growing all around it with pink flowers for the bees. Between the cherry tree and the clammacherry tree was a patch of land just wide enough to play rounders. The yellow house sat right in the belly of the hill, a mound of soft white stone covered with bush, topped with pine trees against the bluest sky with clouds like soft blankets of white cotton wool. Amanda wondered just how old the hill was and what memories it held.

4

Amanda's oldest memory of being in her body was waking to the shouts of "FY-AAHH! FY-AAHH!" in the middle of the night and being dragged out of the house by Gran.

"MURR-DAH!"

Canes cracking, canes marching across the hill.

"FY-AAHH!"

Thelma running for buckets of water and dousing the front of the two-bedroom chattel, while the hose beat down the side of the house.

Gran wailing: "LORD HAVEST MERCY!"

Amanda standing there, like Gran's

noonday shadow, silently willing: *Wind die, wind die.* Feeling the heat of the fire on her skin, Amanda felt fear for the first time in her belly. She could not move.

The sirens sounding long before the fire truck got up the hill to put out one more cane fire at Pleasant Hall. The ashes floating, floating weightless, the hill now a sea of ash; All Saints Church, All Saints Boys' School, Amy's house in the back, the dog house, the galvanized paling, the limestone steps, the Barbados Pride hanging over the edge of the bank, the mahogany tree with roots rising out of the ground like veins on a working man's hands, the fourteen steps of the boys' school, the graves of the dead; black, black, blackness everywhere.

As Pleasant Hall was black, so Mile and a Quarter was full of color. Amanda would sit on the yellow veranda while Gran did her hair in five big plaits that stuck out north, south, east and west, tying two big red ribbons onto the two plaits in the back. Amanda learned to plait and braid quickly so that she would not have to suffer Gran's hairdo for too long.

Some evenings as the sun set, painting the sky in shades of red and orange, Gran would let her practice on her hair. Amanda would ask her everything she wanted to know, and Amanda wanted to know everything. One story she would make Gran repeat over and over was the story of the morning of her birth.

5

You come with lightning and rain at the crack-a-dawn. I remember 'cause I am the one who went for Auntie Joan. I went in the rain in a long sou'wester* cloak; a sou'wester cloak my father left with me when he come from America.

"My father was a sailor. I only see him once in my life. I remember that moment like it was yesterday. When I meet him, it was raining and he was wearing the very said cloak. When he see that I soaking wet, he take off the cloak and put it over my shoulders. His cloak protected me from the cold rain the morning you come, and the lightning showed me the way to Auntie

Joan's house.

"I had to wear the rubber boots I wear in the ground to wade through the water. The rain did falling all through the night washing away all the stuff in the gutters, running down to the sea. The sea did big. I could hear it pounding from Pleasant Hall Hill. I knew you were coming. I pull the sou'wester cloak tight around me and God car' me down Benn Hill to Auntie Joan. She answer me at the first knock.

"Don't get frighten. It is me, I said.

"I know, she called out.

"It is time, Auntie Joan. I going ahead. I said.

"No. She said, *I ready. I'm coming now. Drive up with me.*

"In two-twos she did out with her bag, a big umbrella, and heading for she beetle Volkswagen. I can remember the morning like it was yesterday. The rain did slow down by then, because Auntie Joan didn't even use she umbrella. I thinking this is a sign... Everything is as it should be. The rain clear the way for you, as you will clear the way for others.

"By the time we get to the house Ann water did break, like waterfall, 'til the bed flood way. The pain had she in a state, but Ann didn't want to lie down, so Auntie Joan tell she to squat. I hold she up from behind. The pressure was too much and Ann started to moan from the pain. Auntie Joan tell she is no use crying, save the energy, when she feel the pressure bear down and push.

"Ann bears down on a moan and push with all of she might. Auntie Joan look between Ann's leg with a searchlight and see your head. Ann couldn't take the squatting no more. Auntie Joan help she turn on to all fours like a big cat. Ann pushed and cried out like a wild animal. Auntie Joan received you in her hands.

"*A girl child.* She said. *A girl child.*

"She instructed me to cut the navel string. I cut it. You come with not one strand of hair on your head, bald, completely bald. I couldn't hold back the joy. My first grandchild! I bury your navel string under a Rosemary tree."

By the time Gran finished the story Amanda would have finished her hairdo, five plaits, because that was the only style Gran would allow. Gran would send Amanda for the hand mirror so she could see herself. She was always pleased with Amanda's handiwork.

They would watch the colors of the evening change until darkness came. Amanda would lie between her legs like an overgrown baby. Then they would go inside and listen to the Rediffusion* until bedtime. Gran and Amanda slept in the same bed.

Amanda was convinced that one day she would wake up and find this old woman dead next to her. Sometimes she would wake up and check to see if Gran was still alive and instead she would find Gran anointing her head and singing, or on her knees in fervent prayer. Gran's dream world was real and a source of inspiration for nocturnal activities. Amanda did not always understand Gran's actions, but they impacted on her life.

6

There is a long table laid out with a white lace tablecloth with eight little fires burning bright, but the tablecloth does not burn. She stretches her neck and it seems to go up forever. Her head is above the thick branches and green foliage of trees. She tries to move, but cannot move. Her feet grow roots inside the belly of the earth. Gran reaches out her right hand and sees the tips of tendrils sprouting buds of purple flowers instead of fingers. There is someone coming, but she cannot see who it is. She hears his voice. "Hal that is you? What you doing here Hal? Hal!" *There is no answer...* "Hal!"

Gran realized that she was sitting upright

in her bed calling her brother's name. She felt a presence in the room. It moved past her like a shadow the weight of a breeze. Her body shivered. A dog outside howled. Gran was still. The howling continued. The hair on Gran's arms stood up.

"Hal that is you?"

Gran looked at Amanda lying on her chest, her knees bent under her hips, and buttocks in the air. The sound of Amanda gritting her teeth agitated Gran.

I got to give that child some pomegranate juice for the worms, she thought to herself.

She could not get rid of the feeling that someone was in the room… and the dream.

She called to her daughter Thelma through the thin partition.

"Thelma, Thelma, you sleeping?"

There was no response. She turned her body so that her feet hung over the side of the bed.

"When the spirit call all you can do is answer."

She raised the palm of her right hand above

her head, pressed the palm of her hand to her chest and bowed her head.

"Even your son sweet Jesus suffered on the cross. John 3:16. For God so loved the world that he give his only begotten son, so that whosoever believeth in him shall not perish but have everlasting life."

Gran slipped her feet into slippers at the side of the bed and stood up. She knew what she had to do.

"Thelma get up!" Gran demanded.

"What happened Gran?" Thelma groaned from her sleep.

"Hal was right here. I could smell him." Gran answered, pulling her dress over her head.

"Gran, what you talking about?" Thelma asked in disbelief.

"Yes! He came to me just now. I am going."

"Going?" Thelma pulled her sleepy body upright. "Where you going this early?" It was three o'clock in the morning.

"To my brother's house." Gran answered.

She put some Florida water* in the palm of her hand, inhaled it, anointed her forehead, and rubbed the palms of her hands together. She wrapped her head with a piece of red madras cloth, reached for her bible, the old sou'wester raincoat that was her father's, and unlocked her bedroom door.

"You can't go down there by yourself this time of the morning." Thelma insisted.

"Is me he called Thelma. I got to go." Gran unlocked the side door.

Thelma slid off the side of her bed, slipped on her slippers, unlocked her bedroom door, and walked to the side door.

"Walk good." Thelma said, almost to herself.

Gran was already past the golden apple tree, past the grass where the children played rounders and by the back paling of Auntie Catherine's house with the clammacherry tree and its parasitical coralita pink flower bee vine.

Gran turned, waving at Thelma in the doorway before disappearing in the predawn light.

***

From a distance Gran saw Hal's wife Marjorie, a small woman, leaning in the doorway of the shingled chattel house. Marjorie saw Gran and knew it was her from the rocking of her body to compensate for the severe knocking of the knees and the pain from the arthritis.

Gran was a tall woman, large even, her breasts reaching down over her belly, which was high as if she was in a permanent state of pregnancy. Gran had cared for her brothers and sisters when her mother was working.

She had always been close to Hal, Marjorie thought to herself. *Thank God she coming, but how she knows so quickly?*

Marjorie had lost all sense of time since the moment she first heard Hal groan in his sleep. The bed shook, echoing the tremors of his body as she felt his hands grabbing at her nightgown. A warm wetness washed over the right cheek of her bottom and down her right thigh, as the strong smell of male urine filled the room. Marjorie jumped out of bed. "Hal you alright?" Hal did not answer.

Marjorie turned on the light, but it was too late. Hal lay on the bed, head tilted back, his eyes and mouth opened wide as if at the last moment he had seen everything, but he didn't have a chance to say a word and he had wanted to. The suddenness and irrevocable state of Hal's condition left Marjorie paralyzed. She stood by the bed, watching her husband's stillness in shock. Marjorie shook him in desperation.

"Get up Hal. Stop playing the fool and get up. Hal! Get up!"

She breathed fast and hard. She carefully placed her head on his belly and stared at his chest, waiting for it to rise and fall. She felt cold. Hal's body was still warm.

Hal isn't breathing. I have to go and call someone. Don't worry Marjorie. Hal still here. Hal still here. No. Call somebody. Call Somebody.

Her body started to shake uncontrollably.

Call somebody. I have to go and call somebody.

"I have to go and call somebody."

Marjorie moved away from the metal bedstead. She could see the hard cardboard partition painted pink with a picture of Jesus Christ on the cross hanging in the center.

"I have to go and call somebody."

She was hearing her own voice, but she did not remember it sounding like this. Marjorie looked to see if there was someone else in the room.

Why did he scream out? What did he see? She saw Hal's body on the bed.

"I have to go and call someone."

Marjorie rushed to the front door, undid the bolts at the top and the bottom, unclipped the lock, turned the small knob and opened the door in one move. Not sure which neighbor she would call or what she would say, Marjorie leaned into the side post of the old door. That's when she saw Gran rocking and coming in the early morning air.

It doesn't matter how she knows. Gran coming. Thank you Jesus, Gran coming. The bed shook

Gran and Hal won't get up? I have to wake up Hal before he misses the truck. But Hal won't get up. Something wrong. Gran was floating on air. Closer now. Closer now.

The dog howled. Marjorie started pulling on the plaits of hair on her head, stifling the need to scream.

Now is not the time. Gran coming. The children. Oh God! The children! Her mind spun like a top. Her body felt weightless.

Majorie's back curved, pushing into the side post, her two arms holding on to the other side of the door for support.

Something wrong! Something wrong!

Gran was right on the one-block step at the open door. Marjorie was going to her. Marjorie was falling. Gran was catching Marjorie, holding her up, taking all the weight, bearing her up, letting her heave against her body, letting her release into her with sound that shattered the quiet of the morning. The sound liquefied, and soon the front of Gran's dress was wet with bodily fluids.

The sound shook the entire house awake. All six children stumbled out of the two bedrooms where they slept: Robert, Dennis, Melissa, Diana, Heather and Haley. The words came sudden like rain.

"Hal won't get up. Something wrong. Something wrong, Gran. Hal pee he bed Gran. Call the Doctor. Call the Doctor. Something wrong."

Then Marjorie became aware of the children.

"Your father..." Marjorie's body hung in midair like an unfinished sentence.

Gran went in to see for herself, although she already knew what she would find. Dennis rushed into the bedroom, followed by Robert, Diana, and Melissa. Heather and Haley, the two youngest, claimed Marjorie's hipbones, one on each side. Robert came from the bedroom with Diana leaning on him, sobbing.

"Pappy dead?" she whispered.

"Go and call Doctor Bernard." Gran directed Robert.

Robert slipped on his slippers and moved quickly without changing his night clothes. Marjorie, with Heather and Haley still clinging to her hips, followed Gran into the bedroom.

Gran looked at the empty body on the bed. She knew the doctor was of no use to Hal now. It was the living she would have to look out for. Marjorie's body, heavy with grief, crumbled at the knees. Heather and Haley clung to her at the shoulders now, like anchors on either side, keeping her from letting go of this world.

"Let us pray," Gran said as she held onto the metal frame and lowered her knees to the ground.

7

Eight. I had to be eight when Dennis came to live by Gran. I didn't mind. After all, he is Gran's nephew, Hal's son, my second cousin. Gran always took in family in trouble. Gran got a bed for him and put it in Thelma's bedroom. Thelma hung a curtain around the bed so that she could have privacy.

That year I had a birthday party with ten of my friends. Early that morning I got up, look in the mirror and holler:

"But I don't look any different!"

Gran dress me in my favourite yellow dress, my long yellow socks, put a ribbon in my hair and took a picture for my mother in America, so she could see how I grow. I felt good in my body. I felt happy especially cause Cathy, Sophia and Michelle would be there. Sophia was my best friend. She said she liked coming to my house because she always got a whole leg of chicken for herself, plus what meat was on my plate. At her house she only got the fin from the wing, or mackerel or saltfish.

Gran cooked all day. I helped her make the sandwiches. She had already baked sweet bread and cake with different colors the day before. Gran asked me what I wanted for my birthday and I said a large French Vanilla ice cream. Dennis went to Auntie Joan's shop for the ice cream.

When he came back, I sat down in the gallery and ate it myself. Dennis sat down and watched me eating the ice cream and I did not offer him a spoonful. Gran sat down watching Dennis watching me eat and I did not even look at her. It was my birthday present, my ice cream. I had never had an entire ice cream for myself before. I was in heaven. That night my belly cut me. I spent a long time in the toilet, crying quietly. The party finished early.

The following morning I heard Gran wake up at the crack of dawn, say her morning prayers, and then she left the bedroom. I rolled into Gran's warm spot, permanently sunken with her weight. My belly ached and my bottom felt sore from the night before. Gran turned on the small clock radio in the kitchen. I could hear the announcement of the dead from the small transistor radio Gran kept in the kitchen.

Soon the smell of the strong green tea Gran made for the family every morning reached the bedroom. Hunger sang a song in my belly, but I would not go to the kitchen.

I could hear Gran and Thelma in the kitchen drinking tea, talking, and laughing. Between the laughter I could hear my name. They were laughing at me and the ice cream incident. I felt ashamed. I should have shared the ice cream, then I wouldn't have gotten sick and spent so much time in the toilet. Then the party would have lasted longer. Gran was singing now.

The Lord can move the highest mountain;
He can take your fears away,
There is no power can stand before him...

I listened to the sounds of Thelma taking a bath, smelling the Ponds Cold Cream she used to grease her skin. I heard the door close as she left for work at the Savannah Beach Hotel. I heard the spoons hitting against the metal sink as Gran washed up the morning dishes. Gran sat down with a heave. She pulled on her big black boots one at a time, the big yellow door swung open, and Gran moved around in the yard.

"Amanda. Amanda." Gran called. I pretended not to hear. I refused to follow Gran into the ground to dig cassava for pone. I was ashamed.

I heard the sound of the heavy galvanized gate scraping against the earth and closing again. Gran's small transistor radio faded in the distance. The house was still.

I felt myself falling into a deep sleep. I let myself go.

***

I see myself standing just above the house at Pleasant Hall. There are fields and fields of cane on fire. The burnt orange flames are walking across the wide expanse of fields, crackling like an entire village of women quarrelling. The fire is a giant moving towards me. I cannot run. My feet are glued to the ground.

I can feel its heat inside of my body. I feel an intense pain in my belly and a heavy weight on my chest. The fire is surrounding me. The fire is burning me, burning me. I cannot breathe. I am outside of my body. I am watching my body burn. I open my mouth to scream, but no sound comes.

I wake up. Dennis is on top of me, his hand is over my mouth and… there is a burning between my legs. I try to move but he holds me down. My panty is gone. Dennis is rubbing himself between my legs. It hurts. I try to get up but I can't move. He is choking me. Dennis has this ugly look on his face and there is this nasty, acrid smell.

"Don't say a word about this to anyone," he says, "or they will find you dead."

He gets up and I see his doggy. He pulls up his short pants and says, "Besides, Gran will never believe you."

Then he is gone. I listen to the side door closing behind him. No one is here. My neck and between my thighs hurt and there is this thick, slimy substance on my nook-nook and on the inside of my thighs. I go to the toilet to pee. My urine burns the inside of my nook-nook. I try to wipe myself with toilet paper but it is too painful. I start to cry. I open my legs to look at it. It is red and bruised and there are little tears in the delicate pink flesh. How can I tell Gran this about my private parts?

Fresh tears gather in my eyes. I cannot stop them flowing. I remember the women under the guava tree doing smocking, whispering about the times of the plantation, and how the slave owners would interfere with the black women in the night. But I did not quite understand what it meant until now.

I go to the kitchen, open the back door and look towards the ground. Gran is coming. I can see her rocking and coming, rocking like a ship in the sea. She opens the big galvanized yard gate. I walk to the edge of the top step.

"You finally wake up?" Gran asks, moving towards the shed to put down the hoe.

"Dennis interfere with me!" I blurt out.

"What!?" Gran shouts.

"Dennis interfere with me."

"Lie!"

"He lay down on top of me."

"Lie!"

"Yes Gran."

"What you do Amanda?"

"I don't know Gran. I was dreaming and when I wake up I find Dennis on top of me and now my nook-nook hurting me."

"Lord havest Mercy!"

Tears fill Gran's eyes as her bladder

releases warm liquid down her legs and into her garden boots.

I watch Gran holding her belly and I am sorry for the pain I have caused her. I want to disappear.

8

You think he would do something so Auntie Joan?"

"What the child tell you Gran?"

"She says he lay down on top of her."

"If that is what the child says, then that is what happened."

"But he's my brother's son."

"Cousins bring monkeys by the dozens."

"Oh God! Auntie Joan, in my house?! What's everybody going say?"

"Don't worry about the people and make your pressure go up. She crossed the red sea yet?"

"No."

"Carry her to the doctor."

"What about the boy Auntie Joan?"

"He smell he piss and it smell rank, put he out."

"I pack he things already. He can't live here no more."

"You look at her Gran?"

"I can't bring myself to look; but she bathe."

"She wash away the evidence."

"Evidence? Oh God. You mean… you think he…?"

"It is very possible… You call the police?"

"I can't put her through that, Auntie Joan."

"She went through the worst already Gran."

"It's the talk I can't take."

"You talk to her?"

"I sent for you as soon as I hear."

"Times changing. You have to talk to her."

"And tell her what?"

"The truth."

"But she not ready yet."

"Whether or not she is ready it here, we got to face it head on.

"Oh God! Auntie Joan."

"I know it hard, but she is a strong girl. I know she from she born."

"What I going tell she mother?"

"The truth. Always tell the truth."

"But she left her in my care."

"You did the best you could. Come Gran, call the doctor. She needs to be examined."

"I know. But she is resting."

"God doesn't send more than you can bear."

"It is true, Auntie Joan. It is true."

Amanda listened through the partition to the whispers of Gran and Auntie Joan speaking about her. She could hear fear in Gran's voice.

She put on a pair of jeans and her favorite t-shirt and walked up the side of Mount Brevitor Hill to the rock of Gibraltar. She looked out beyond the houses to the sea.

She leaned against the root of the tall mile tree. She wondered what would happen to her now. What did Dennis do to her? Why did Auntie Joan want to call the police? What would happen to her now? Would the police take her away from Gran?

Amanda felt hot and giddy. The trade winds blew gently against her skin, cooling her. She could sense the water coming in the wind. Too tired to move, Amanda lay on her back looking up at the sky, so big and wide. She could see the bright clouds moving away and dark clouds moving over her.

The rain started to trickle down from the clouds drop by drop, until it found a steady rhythm. *This is a passing shower*, Amanda thought. It was cold and sweet.

And then it began beating her body like a drum; a polyrhythm of raindrops, forcing a wrenching sound from her belly. It felt like her belly was caving in on itself. She held onto herself, pulling her body into a ball, crawling between two roots of the tree which embraced her like comforting arms.

Soothed by the sound of the falling rain water beating against her body, Amanda closed her eyes and slipped into the stream of light behind her eyelids. In the nothingness she could hear a woman chanting. She could see her now, with a bag of bones, chanting and dancing right in front of her. She touched the bag of bones against the center of Amanda's forehead, her chest, her belly, the palms of her hands and the bottoms of her feet. The woman anointed Amanda's head with sweet smelling oil and tied a cloth the color of red earth on her head. It smelled older than Gran.

Amanda was chanting with the woman with bones, her heart racing. She led Amanda to a hole big enough to hold one body. Amanda stood in the hole. It was just deep enough that her head was above the ground.

The woman threw red earth into the hole until it was full. Amanda tried to move, but she could not. She became afraid. She screamed and found herself in her body at the root of the mile tree. The rain had stopped. Amanda watched new clouds, wisps of white foam floating in blue skies, passing over her going towards the sea.

The trade wind caused her to shiver slightly

as it touched the shirt against her skin. She got up and spread her arms wide, letting the heat of the sun's rays warm her body. She looked at the mile tree where she had just sat. It was so tall and thin that it seemed like if you climbed it you could reach heaven. But she was afraid of heights. She preferred the roots. She felt the root of the tree with the palm of her hand, remembering the woman with the bones. It felt so real, but all she tried, she could not remember the words of the chant.

"AMANDA! AMANDA!" Gran's voice called her with a sense of urgency.

"Coming!" Amanda answered instantly. "Coming!!"

9

Amanda went to the doctor and had a check-up. Nothing more was said about what happened. The bed was removed from Auntie Thelma's room and Dennis returned to his mother Marjorie's house.

Gran watched Amanda like a hawk. She would not let her out of her sight, except for school. Amanda could no longer wear short pants outside of the house. Gran would not let her go running on the pasture. Instead she had to invite her friends to the house to play school, snakes and ladders, or sing songs on the gallery.

Most of the time Amanda retreated to her bedroom, creating a tent in the corner between the clothing closet and the window with a blanket. She would sit quietly underneath this haven for hours, crocheting small circular worlds of color and undoing them, making them over and over again, like the pattern of repetition the woman with bones sang in the world under the mile tree.

She had no words for her feelings. Sometimes tears would come from nowhere, but no words. She wanted to return to the world of the woman with bones; return to the nothingness.

Somebody wanted her to come here, now, in this time, in this house. Amanda was told that when she was in her mother's womb her mother drank paw-paw leaves but she did not bleed. She was told that her father beat her mother and disowned her. They say he left on a plane to America. He never came back. She did not know what her mother looked like. They say she left when Amanda was a baby to go and live with her big sister Gloria in America. She left no photograph.

Amanda was told that one day her mother

would send for her.

Now there was this secret that made her hide, and she did not understand why she had to hide. It was not her fault. She did not want to be here, in this room, in this silence, in this body.

10

Amanda's feet took her skipping as fast as she could past the clammacherry tree sea monster clinging onto the back paling of Auntie Catherine's house. Amanda always ran past the old house, shut up and falling in on itself, afraid that Auntie Catherine's spirit would appear suddenly and take her heart. Once Amanda passed the old house, she felt safe.

It was only recently that Gran let her go to Auntie Joan by herself, and only when there was no other option. Gran made her tie the money and the list in a handkerchief before pinning it to the tab of her jeans, and stuffing it in her right front pocket. At least she didn't have to stuff it down her chest, because she had nothing to hold it in. Amanda could not imagine herself wearing one of those big bras with metal that Gran wore.

She was always the one that stood behind Gran, pulling each side of the wide brassiere, fastening it from the lowest metal fastener to the highest metal fastener until all of the flesh was sealed in tight. Gran would stand there, sweat dripping from her face with the effort it took to get dressed. She would put her vest over her bra, her dress over her vest, put her money in a handkerchief, tie it, and stuff it in her bra on top of her breast.

God, I hope I never have to walk around squeezed inside my clothes like that, Amanda silently prayed.

She looked at the pin in the tab of her pants and heard Gran's voice in her head: "Better safe than sorry." Gran did the same thing to her every day when she went to school. Gran would tie her pocket money in a handkerchief and pin it to the inside of the side pocket of her red overall. Amanda went along with it, until one day while standing in a circle of girls around Merle's tray, Amanda pulled out the handkerchief and started to untie it. Jackie saw the pin and hollered out.

"Look how Amanda uniform pin up like a big able diaper!"

Laughter spread through the circle as every girl turned and looked at Amanda as she tugged and pulled at Gran's knot.

Jackie squealed: "And she money in a handkerchief."

The laughter closed in on Amanda. She couldn't move. No words would come. "Wha' happen? You grandmother can't afford a purse?"

Jackie pulled out a multi-colored beaded purse from her red overall.

"Made in Japan," she said as she smacked her tongue against the roof of her mouth, closing and opening her eyes in timing while unzipping the purse. The entire group went quiet. Amanda said nothing.

"Try and leave the girl." Sophia commanded.

Amanda turned and saw Sophia by her right shoulder. She didn't know where she came from or when she got there, but Amanda was glad she was there. Jackie did a snake dance, her body sliding on air from her head through her shoulders, gliding from her waist to her hips and into her legs, shifting her weight from one side to the other, finishing the sparring action with her hip bone jutting out and her eyes focused for the kill.

"You better don't touch me! Cause you would see!" The words squirted from Jackie's mouth like venom.

"Fight! Fight!" Someone in the crowd shouted. The girls closest to Jackie, Amanda, and Sophia stepped back to give them room.

"Fight! Fight!" Another voice echoed.

Everyone waited to see what was going to happen next. Sophia grabbed Amanda by the elbow and pulled her through the small crowd around Merle's tray. The girls parted like the red sea making a path for the Israelites. The two girls walked through, turning their heads to see if Jackie would follow.

"She like she know." Jackie said out loud, "she like she know to step off! Causing she can't touch me and talk! I would lick in she tail!!!"

Jackie made a whipping sound with the tips of the two fingers next to her thumb, sucked air through her teeth, batted her eyelids and shook her hips for everyone to see she had things under control.

Amanda and Sophia were drawn to Merle's tray by the smell of ginger and nutmeg. Amanda leaned her head forward and took a deep breath. Amanda's mouth was already watering, tasting the warm, soothing sweetness of Merle's sugar cake.

"Two twenty-five cent portions of sugar cake please." Amanda said, finding her voice, coins triumphantly jingling in her fisted hand.

The school girls in their red tunics with their hushed tones and whispered glances, a sea of bodies, rushed in to regain their spaces behind Amanda and Sophia, washing away Jackie's threats of destruction. Merle placed a piece of thick brown paper in each of the girls' hands and spooned heavy loads of warm, syrupy coconut sweetness onto the center of the paper.

"Thank you." Amanda said as she placed fifty cents in the palm of Merle's hand.

Merle's sugar cake is the best. Amanda thought to herself.

"I know." Merle said. Her voice was deep and rich and touched her on her back like warm water on a cool morning.

Amanda was shocked. How did Merle know what she was thinking? Amanda squeezed her eyebrows down and together like her Gran did sometimes in the middle of a story. Merle placed the two silver quarters back in Amanda's hand.

"This one is for you," she said.

"Thank you," Amanda said.

"Thank you," Sophia echoed.

The two girls sat under the tamarind tree on the pasture dipping their fingers into the soft, gooey sugar cake. Amanda loved sitting under the tree with Sophia. She felt they were made from the same piece of cloth. They hardly spoke when eating and the silence was a comfort.

Amanda heard a bicycle bell. She looked up and saw Old Man Mortimer with coconut brooms passing. She had been lost in the memory of Jackie and the handkerchief scene. Her mouth watered. She wondered if Merle had any sugar cake at her house. She would have to wait until Monday. If she went for sugar cake and Gran found out, she would be punished for not walking the straight road.

Since that incident, Amanda always unpinned her handkerchief in the bathroom before going to Merle's tray. She looked at the huge pin on her pants tab. Now Gran expected her to wear a big able pin to Auntie Joan's shop.

Look at it, it look like something to pin up a baby diaper in truth.

She had enough hiding and unpinning.

Best time to do it was now.

She took the small yellow and red crocheted purse she made herself from her left pocket, took the money and the list from the handkerchief, placed it in her purse and tied the string. She had to make sure that the purse was secure in one of her pants pockets and the pin and the handkerchief in the other pants pocket before beginning her journey up Mile and a Quarter main road. When she returned she would remember to pin the handkerchief exactly as Gran did it on her right pocket, and hide the crocheted sack.

Amanda sang out loud:

> *I say B*
> *I say B*
> *I say BA*
> *BA*
> *BAR*
> *BAR*
> *BARB*
> *BARB*
> *BARBADOS*

BARBADOS

I say I…

Amanda sang loud enough that Mr. Bailey looked out of his louvers, his glasses perched on the tip of his nose as if he was really looking over them and not through them. His brown almond eyes moved quickly from side to side surveying the road before resting on Amanda perched on the trunk of the tree directly across the street.

"Good morning Mr. Bailey," Amanda said.

Mr. Bailey moved to the open window. He eased first his shoulder and then his upper torso through the opening.

"Good morning Amanda," he answered, "you singing sweet enough this morning."

"Thank you Mr. Bailey." Amanda answered in her best voice. "I'm practicing for the independence program."

"You start early?"

"Yes please."

Mr. Bailey's fingers moved to his face just in time to stop his glasses from sliding off his nose. He did this without disturbing the silver thimble on the finger of one of his hands and the needle with thread in his other hand.

"Me? I could never perform on stage, too nervous. But you young lady, you are very brave."

She looked at the ground, avoiding Mr. Bailey's eyes.

"I get nervous too Mr. Bailey."

"And how is Gran this morning?"

"Fine thank you. I got to go. Gran waiting for me to come back." Amanda said, turning to run.

"Take your time and be careful crossing the road now."

"Yes please."

"And when you return collect Gran's newspaper."

"Yes Mr. Bailey." Amanda answered, walking away while holding back the urge to run.

Mr. Bailey pushed his glasses back up on his nose before pulling his head and upper body back in through the window.

Amanda wondered how long Mr. Bailey had been watching her. If Gran knew that she untied the money before getting to the shop, Gran would quarrel. Gran had never beaten her before. But she hated having the money pinned to her like some little baby. She was almost nine already. It wasn't her fault that her mother left her with an old woman.

Mr. Bailey won't tell Gran, after all, he's an educated man. Gran says educated people don't have time to malicious in people business, they're too busy with business of their own.

Amanda skipped past the bus stop with the sign saying 'Out of City'. The smell of Rosalyn's mother's coconut turnovers made Amanda stop and inhale. "Rosalyn!" Amanda shouted as she turned the corner and stepped onto the side steps of the house. Rosalyn's mother Tantie's eyes and ears appeared at the glass louvers of the side door.

"Good Morning Tantie."

"Morning Amanda, and how are you this

morning?"

"Fine thanks."

"And Gran?"

"She good. Rosalyn home?"

"She went by her Godmother. You're going home now?"

"No please, I'm going by Auntie Joan's shop."

"When you come back from the shop, stop for some turnovers."

"Yes please," Amanda answered, wishing she could have one now.

"Now be careful walking the road." Tantie warned before turning away from the louvers and hustling back to the kitchen to check on her turnovers in the oven.

"Yes please."

Amanda turned on her heels and climbed onto the black and white striped bridge like a zebra's back, taking one step at a time while trying not to look down into the gully with its forgotten river bed. The height excited her, yet there was this fear that she would fall and not only hurt herself, but she hated the thought that she could become dirty with the mud and soft breadfruit with flies nesting on their yellow, decaying flesh.

She jumped from the zebra-striped bridge and onto the sidewalk and began moving quickly. She ran past the black belly sheep grazing on green grass and pausing to chew, past the big house with all the tractors outside waiting for cane season, until she came to the piece of earth like a woman's behind jutting into the road.

She crossed over to the other side of the road, avoiding walking around the blind corner, and then she ran again, past the chattel houses on the bank of stone, past the gas station where the old man sat drinking a Banks beer, pausing to look left and right before she crossed the road that led to Maynard Road.

She ran slightly uphill to the door of Auntie Joan's shop, made a sharp turn into the doorway, almost knocking down Mrs. Braithwaite who was about to exit the shop with her bag full of goods. Mrs. Braithwaite stumbled off balance. It was a good thing that Auntie Joan was right behind her to stop her from falling.

"Sorry Mrs. Braithwaite," Amanda panted.

Mrs. Braithwaite placed her vinyl bag bursting with groceries back on the counter with a look of impatience on her face.

"You alright?" Auntie Joan asked Mrs. Braithwaite.

"You need to be more careful young lady." Mrs. Braithwaite scolded Amanda.

"Yes please. I real sorry I…"

"You said so already," Mrs. Braithwaite interrupted her before she could say anything more.

"Mrs. Braithwaite let me bring you a chair. Sit down and catch yourself," Auntie Joan offered as she moved a chair from behind the counter for her. "You want a glass of water?"

"No thank you." Mrs. Braithwaite responded.

Auntie Joan led Amanda to the counter. Amanda pulled the list from her crocheted purse. 2 lbs. of salt fish, a pint of peas, and a cake of blue soap. Auntie Joan weighed the salt fish and wrapped it in brown paper, measured a pint of peas in the tin measuring cup, put them in a small brown paper bag and placed the blue soap in its own small brown paper bag separate from the peas.

Auntie Joan took the money from Amanda and gave her the change. Amanda put the change in her crocheted purse and placed it carefully in her pocket. She put the goods in her handbag and said, "Thanks Auntie."

"Now you be careful walking the road Amanda," Auntie Joan warned.

"Alright Auntie, but I was just running." Amanda answered.

"And stop all the running."

"Yes please." Amanda looked down at the wooden floor, ashamed of her behavior.

Auntie Joan reached into the larder where the ham and cheese lay sliced and waiting to be placed in salt bread for ham cutters and cheese cutters, with the bowl of hot sauce and a bowl with ketchup on one level, and on the other level trays of homemade sweets. She took a piece of black bitch candy from one of the trays, wrapped it in brown paper and placed it Amanda's hand, rubbing and kneading the hand as if she was passing more than the sweet.

Amanda picked up her bag from the counter and moved towards the doorway.

Mrs. Braithwaite moved towards Auntie Joan, leaning the top half of her body over the counter while keeping her eyes on Amanda.

"Who that race horse belongs to?"

"That is Mrs. Wilson granddaughter. Ann's girl child." Auntie Joan answered proudly.

Mrs. Braithwaite looked puzzled.

"Really, the girl that went away and left the baby? Ooooh! That is she. The children these days growing up real fast. I didn't even recognize her."

Amanda heard Auntie Joan and Mrs. Braithwaite whispering. She could feel their eyes on her back. She felt a knot in her belly. Something bad was going to happen.

She took her time and walked down the

road carefully, avoiding the high bridge, stopping to collect the turnovers from Tantie, stopping to collect Gran's newspaper from Mr. Bailey, stopping under the tree to hide her crocheted purse and transfer the change and the list to the white handkerchief and pin it to her pocket with the big-able pin.

The turnovers from Tantie were hot. She could smell the coconut with cinnamon, sugar and essence through the wrapping and the brown paper bag.

When she got home, Gran was pleased with her. She had bought everything on the list and brought back the change. Gran gave her two turnovers with a glass of cold mauby. Amanda ate them slowly. She could not get rid of the feeling that something bad was going to happen.

11

"Wrapping round
dipping in pulling out
turning round and pulling through,
wrapping round
dipping in pulling out
turning round and pulling through
making something new

red red red red
round and round and round and round
curling up and curling down
making something new

wrapping round
dipping in pulling out
turning round and pulling through
wrapping round

dipping in pulling out
turning round and pulling through
making something new

yellow yellow yellow
round and round and round and round
curling up and curling down
making something new

wrapping round
dipping in pulling out
turning round and pulling through
wrapping round
dipping in pulling out
turning round and pulling through
making something new"

"Amanda! Amanda!"

"red red red red
round and round and round and round
curling up and curling down
making something new

wrapping round
dipping in pulling out
turning round and pulling through

wrapping round
dipping in pulling out
turning round and pulling through
making something new."

"Amanda! Amanda!"

"Cheesed-on brothers!" Amanda lost her rhythm. The urgency in Gran's voice forced Amanda's hands to stop crocheting.

"Yes Gran!"

"Come out here now!" Gran hollered.

"Just when I was getting into it," Amanda said to herself.

Gran's voice sounded serious. Amanda wrapped the beautiful red and yellow center piece she was crocheting around the two balls of wool, pushed her silver crochet needle through the ball and placed the bundle under the tent in her corner of the room. She rushed to the veranda.

Amanda could hear a woman's voice from the outside. It sounded familiar, but she wasn't sure who it was. She peeped through the side window and saw Mrs. Braithwaite under the golden apple tree, her mouth pushed up in the air, indicating her state of distress. Gran was standing next to her with a thin tamarind rod* in her right hand and her left hand on her waist like she was performing the 'I'm the little teapot' song.

Gran find out about the handkerchief. But why is Mrs. Braithwaite here? How would she know about the handkerchief? Amanda thought to herself. *Oh no! She told her I was running on the road.*

"AMANDA!"

The intensity in Gran's voice made Amanda pause with her hand on the front door handle. She opened the door quietly, closed it behind her, and leaned against it.

"Yes Gran?" Her answer was barely audible.

"You speak to Mrs. Braithwaite?"

The look on Gran's face made Amanda

pull her body in and straighten up so that she took up as little space as possible.

Gran definitely knows about the handkerchief and running on the road, she thought. She wished she could slip through a crack in the earth into another world.

"Good afternoon, Mrs. Braithwaite." Amanda mumbled.

"Good afternoon." Mrs. Braithwaite shifted her weight from side to side and looked down her nose at Amanda from her head to her toe and back up to her head again.

"Amanda did you curse Mrs. Braithwaite?" Gran inquired.

Amanda's mouth dropped open in surprise. She shook her head no.

"Don't shake your head at me. Open your mouth and answer me when I am speaking to you."

Amanda's mouth widened in shock.

"Answer me girl. You want to catch flies?"

Amanda closed her mouth and dropped her chin to her chest. She looked down at her bare feet. Amanda felt a lump growing in her throat. She shook her head no.

"Don't shake your head at me!" Gran shouted, "and open your mouth and talk."

Amanda stared at Mrs. Braithwaite. If looks could kill, Mrs. Braithwaite would have dropped down dead in that instant.

Why is she doing this to me? Amanda's mind raced.

"Yes! That is the child that curse me in her school new-niform." Mrs. Braithwaite pointed her index finger at Amanda.

"Amanda I asking you for the second time, did you curse Mrs. Braithwaite?" Gran's face tightened in anguish.

Amanda turned her head from side to side, sucking in the feeling of fear. Teardrops gathered like a peaking tidal wave at the rims of her eyelids. Shifting her weight to her right leg, she rubbed the bottom of her left foot up and down on her right calf.

"Stand up properly!" Gran shouted.

"As God is my witness," Mrs. Braithwaite kissed the palm of her hand, turned it over, kissed the back of her hand and raised her palm to the sky. "This child curse me stink with bad words a few days ago. If not for the new-niform I would not have believed she was a school child. Tell you the truth I know the face, but I would not have known she was Ann girl if I had not seen her by Auntie Joan's shop the other day. When I find out that she was your grandchild I could not believe it, causing I know you is a God-fearing woman. That is why I come here this evening. I know you would want to know. She ran before I catch her. If I did catch her as God is my witness I would have skin she backside personally."

Amanda backed away from the two women.

"She wants to run. Don't let she run!" Mrs. Braithwaite shouted before Gran could say a word.

"I not running, I…" Amanda shouted back.

"You got mout' now!" Mrs. Braithwaite interjected, "now you got mout'! The young people too disrespectful, you have to tame them 'fore it's too late."

Gran grabbed Amanda by her shoulder and shook her.

"Girl, who you shouting at? You got nuff mout' now, but when I ask you a question you can't answer me? You mother left you here and I try my best with you. I raise you to curse big people? Huh... Answer me that! I raise you to curse? You ever see me cursing 'bout here?"

The tidal wave peaked and its water flooded Amanda's face.

Gran leaned forward, her face angry like ants in a stirred up nest.

"Amanda did you curse Mrs. Braithwaite?"

"NO GRAN!" The words flew out of her mouth loud and sharp.

"Don't raise your voice at me Amanda. Mrs. Braithwaite right here. She see you with she own two eyes. Are you lying Amanda? It is one thing to have a filthy mouth, but it is another thing to be a liar, Amanda. A liar cannot be trusted. What else have you lied about?"

The tears were unstoppable. Amanda

repeatedly wiped away the flood of tears with desperation. First her right cheek with her right hand, then her left cheek with her left hand.

"Don't cry or I will give you something to cry about. Speak the truth."

Gran shook the tamarind rod in Amanda's face. Amanda's breathing was jagged and panicked. She had never been beaten with a tamarind rod before, but she had heard about its sting.

"I want satisfaction." Mrs. Braithwaite interjected. "Spare the rod and spoil de child."

The first sting across the back of both her legs took Amanda by surprise. She did a little skip and a hop, holding her hands like a protective shield down the side of her body, sucking in breath through her mouth in response to the agony at the moment of the sting of the whip on her flesh.

"Don't!_Tell!_Lies!"

Each word that Gran shouted she accented with a lash. Amanda started to skip to the rhythm, lifting her legs in agony.

"Don't let she pull you down Mrs. Wilson."
Mrs. Braithwaite warned.

Gran hoisted Amanda up by the center of
the back of her pants. Amanda's body hung
like a puppet dangling from a marionette's
string.

"Don't!_Tell!_Lies! Don't!_Tell!_Lies!"

"Don't!_Tell!_Lies! Don't!_Tell!_Lies!"

Gran's demonstrative cries impressed Mrs.
Braithwaite, who stood with a look of pride
on her face.

Sophia, her grandmother, Michelle and
Cathy came running down the gap to see
what all the commotion was about.

Amanda stopped her dance. She sucked in
a scream quivering in her belly and started
listening to herself.

*Don't let them see you screaming, stay still,
stay still… still… still, silence, one day you will
grow bigger, leave here, and never have to see
these people again.*

Amanda had seen photographs of *Bloody
Sunday in Selma* on a program about Martin

Luther King. All the black people were running and the white policemen with masks were beating them. Some lowered their bodies and covered their heads with their arms. She covered her head, bent her knees and lowered her body to the ground.

Gran's hands stopped in midair. Her entire body, at first frozen with intention, melted as she lost the will to strike the child. Nobody said a word.

Amanda crawled away on all fours, got onto her knees, then onto her feet and, weak in the knees, wobbled up the steps and into the house. She stood in the small bedroom she shared with Gran. Her whole body trembled at the thought of what just happened. She had never been beaten before.

She crawled into a corner and sat, but sitting hurt. She looked at her legs. There were snakes along the sides and backs of her legs. Touching them hurt. She imagined that this must be how you felt after a war.

She crawled out of the corner and onto the bed. She remembered Dennis and what he had done to her in this bed. At least he was gone, and now this. Why did Gran believe this woman?

Amanda started to sob from deep in her belly. The sobs shook her entire body. She cried until she fell asleep. She slept for the rest of the day.

12

G od come for your world."

Gran looked up in the air, right hand reaching for the ceiling, and waited as if she expected God to descend at that moment and take what was his.

"The Israelites were in bondage for generations before you send Moses, don't forget your people in the Caribbean Sea.

"Amanda child, now plane crashing right in Buhbadus waters. Terrorism! I wonder who is the terrorist?"

Gran held the newspaper up, looking at the pictures of the bodies covered with black plastic material and the fragments of the plane found in the water.

Amanda took her time coming from the bedroom. She still had not forgiven Gran, but she came. She had never heard of a plane crashing in Barbados waters. She looked over Gran's shoulder and read in her best classroom voice.

"The Cubana de Aviacion Flight 455 Boeing 367 landed at Seawell International Airport for refueling early this morning en route to Jamaica. Eleven minutes after take-off, eight km west of Barbados, the plane crashed in the Caribbean Sea. All seventy-eight people on board the Douglas DC-8 aircraft were killed."

"May their souls rest in peace." Gran prayed.

"Why Gran? Everybody dead? Just so? 78 people dead?"

"When I was a girl, there was a hungry black man, I don't recall his name. One day he was passing through Strathclyde. Now Strathclyde was a posh neighborhood and at that time no black people use to live there. As a matter of fact no black people use to walk through Strathclyde. It was an unspoken law. The only black people walking through Strathclyde were the maids and the gardeners.

"This hungry black man in question was taking risk causing he was so hungry. You see Strathclyde was a shortcut he never took. He was walking quickly through Strathclyde and all he could smell is ripe julie mangoes, then he see the tree laden with julie mangoes, mangoes under the tree rottening, mangoes in the gutter where the water does run off to the sea rottening.

"The hungry black man belly start to growl like a wild beast, sending a message to the hungry black man brain. When that did not work, he belly send a message to his throat to find out if he throat cut. He forgot his mother's training. So he tiptoe to the fence, peep round. He did not see anyone.

"The hungry black man walk through the gate and climb the mango tree. He pick two ripe mangoes, put them in his pockets and hurry down out of the tree. The owner of the house happened to peep out of the window, see the hungry black man coming down from the tree, and shoot him before he walk out the gate. The hungry black man fell down dead."

"But why Gran? Why he shoot him for two mangoes Gran?"

"Because he could." Gran paused, "and even more so because of fear."

"But it is not fair, the mangoes were wasting when the man was hungry." Amanda interrupted.

"Remember, to the man in the house the man in the tree is a thief; a black man who was a thief in a neighborhood that don't want black people there is in a dangerous position."

"He dead because he was a black man Gran? And what this got to do with the plane?"

"Everything is connected, one way or the other. Who is the terrorist? The man with the gun or the man in the tree?"

Gran paused. Amanda was silent for a

moment then she blurted out: "The man with the gun that did wasting the mangoes. He shoot the man because he was black and a thief."

Gran smiled. "Go and shut the windows in the house."

"Gran nuh rain falling."

"I smell the rain coming in the wind."

"Alright."

Amanda walked from the veranda into the living room, through the two bedrooms and into the kitchen, shutting the windows as she passed through each room. Her body still had a slight ache from the beating.

She had decided she was never speaking to Gran again. But when Gran showed her the newspaper with the dead bodies she could not keep that promise to herself. Gran could not read. She always read the newspaper to Gran. It was her duty.

By the time she got to the back door she could see the heavy clouds over Mount Brevitor Hill. It was already raining on the hill, but in the valley where the yellow house stood, the earth waited patiently. Amanda watched the rain walking down the acre of land between the hill and the yellow house. Then she walked back to the gallery where Gran sat.

"You alright?" Gran asked.

"Yeah."

"You sure?"

"Yes, Gran."

"This thing with Dennis you know it's not your fault."

"What you mean Gran?"

"I don't want you to feel bad, to blame yourself. He was wrong. These things have been happening for a long time on the island. My mother had thirteen children, all from different fathers. She said she was first taken by her uncle."

Gran paused.

"I wanted to protect you from all that. That is why I took you everywhere with me. But look how it happen… right inside the house, right inside the bed where I does sleep."

Gran looked out to the horizon. By now

the rain was beating on the galvanized roof, walking over the house to the gallery.

"When I was your age, all we had was a one room chattel. All of we in one room, no bigger than a slave hut. Every morning we had to walk to the stand pipe to catch water. There was no school. You had to have money to go to school. Only hard work for me. Things different now. Education free now; the Skipper see to that. You can read and write. You have the opportunity to go places and do things I never knew existed. This house, me, everything that happened here, will come to pass. It will become what you make of it."

"But Gran why? Why he do that?"

"Because he could. He living in fear too. He not right."

"Dennis hurt me Gran."

"Shhhh! I know. He can't hurt you anymore.

"You hurt me too Gran."

"I know." Gran said.

"And I didn't do it Gran, I didn't do it."

"I know."

"So why you beat me in front of everybody?"

"I'm sorry."

Gran eyes filled with tears threatening to flood her face. Amanda had never seen Gran cry before. Gran opened her mouth to speak, but spastic sounds replaced words and then a moan came. Her big belly shook in spasms as she lost control of the liquids in her body. Water ran from her eyes, from her nose, and spittle sprayed from the corner of her mouth. Gran wiped the corner of her mouth and stopped trying to speak.

Amanda crawled into Gran's lap and held her until her body stopped shaking. Then she lay between Gran's legs, feeling like she was growing too big for Gran's lap, knowing that one day she would leave this place, seek the world and live unafraid.

The rain was heavy now, the wind bending the trees. By now it had reached the sea. Gran cradled Amanda in her lap as if she was a baby again and rocked her. Amanda's tears were heavy like the rain.

"This too will pass." Gran whispered in Amanda ears.

"This too will pass." Amanda echoed. "This too will pass."

Glossary

Florida water

an American version of Eau de Cologne, or Cologne Water. It has the same citrus basis as Cologne Water, but shifts the emphasis to sweet orange (rather than the lemon and neroli of the original Cologne Water), and adds spicy notes including lavender and clove

Rediffusion

a British business (Broadcast Relay Sevice Inc.) which distributed radio and TV signals through wired relay networks. The first British colony to have the Rediffusion service was Barbados in 1934, when Radio Distribution (Barbados) Limited was formed

sou'wester

a storm or gale blowing from the southwest

tamarind rod

a small, flexible whip made from a slender branch of the tamarind tree and used for corporal punishment

About the Author

Photo by Rachelle Gray

Sonia S. Williams is a Performance Artist, Theatre Director, Writer, an Educator in Theatre Arts, Inspirational Speaker and Activist.

Born January 17th in 1967 at Pleasant Hall, St. Peter, Sonia migrated to Brooklyn New York in 1979 where she attended Brooklyn Technical High School and Hamilton College, Clinton, New York. There she received a B.A. in Theatre Arts and Women's Studies and a Watson Fellowship to Nigeria 1989. Since she returned to Barbados in 1990, she has acted extensively under the direction of Earl Warner, in her one-woman plays, and as a performance poet. Sonia has performed as a dancer on the hotel circuit, sang backup for a fusion with jazz performer Blak Klay Soyl and El Vernon Del Congo and can be seen in the Canadian film *The Triangle* and the Barbadian feature film *Sweet Bottom*.

Sonia has written and directed full length plays including: *Amandala* and *The Ritual*, one woman pieces *3 Points Off Center* and Pilgrimage to *Freedom* and the choreopoem *Embodied Knowings*. Sonia is the recipient of many awards including the Karen Williams Prize in Theatre 1988, The Actress of the year Barbados 1990, The Governor General Award for excellence in Drama in the professional category of the National Independence Festival of the Creative Arts 1999.

She has taught extensively in the English-speaking Caribbean including at the Edna Manley College for the Visual and Performing Arts in Jamaica, Youth Training Entrepreneurship Scheme in Trinidad, Garrison Secondary School, the Barbados Youth Service and the Barbados Community College, and in the BFA in Creative Arts at the University of the West Indies, Cave Hill. Sonia has completed a Post-Graduate degree in Higher Education Teaching and Learning at the University of the West Indies.

She is regarded as one of the most important

of a younger generation of directors working in Caribbean theatre today. Her credits include *Odale's Choice, Return to the Source,* (excerpts from *Mask*) written by Kamau Braithwaite, *Children of Negus* with writings from Kamau and Bruce St. John and *Shepherd* by Rawle Gibbons of Trinidad and Tobago. She has directed works for National events for the Commission for Pan-African Affairs and the Prime Minister's office and represented the country at Carifesta, as a writer, director and performer. She has dramaturged work for various groups and has facilitated youth development using theatre in Communities in Barbados.

Sonia participated in the 1998 Writer's Workshop in Poetry UWI Cave Hill, and the 2001 Writer's Workshop in Fiction UWI Cave Hill. She was a writer-in-residence at The Cropper Foundation Creative Writers Residential Workshop, Trinidad in 2012. She has performed her writings extensively as a solo artist. She has published a short story and poetry in *POUI*.

She has three children and one grandchild and lives on the West Coast of the island, maintaining a close relationship with the sea. She is a vegetarian who practices Reiki. Her intention is to facilitate the development of people and the transformation of lives through artistic excellence and service.

Contact

(246) 822-6286
omisola46@gmail.com
5TH AVENUE DURANT VILLAGE
HOLDERS HILL
ST JAMES
BARBADOS